1.7

For
Nanna Betty Rosa & Grandma Shirley
with love

Published in 2010 by Windmill Books, LLC
303 Park Avenue South, Suite # 1280, New York, NY 10010-3657

Adaptations to North American Edition © 2010 Windmill Books
Text copyright © 2004 Alan Bowater
Illustrations copyright © Pete Pascoe

Originally published by JoJo Publishing
"Yarra's Edge"
2203/80 Lorimer Street
Docklands VIC 3008
Australia

In conjunction with Purple Pig Productions

CREDITS:
Text by Alan Bowater
Illustrated by Pete Pascoe
Designed by Pete Pascoe, Alan Bowater, and Rob Ryan

Publisher Cataloging Data

Bowater, Alan
  A pig called Pete. – North American ed. / written by Alan Bowater ; illustrated by Pete Pascoe.
       p.   cm. – (A pig called Pete)
  Summary: Pete is no ordinary pig; he's purple instead of pink, he likes to take baths, and every night he flies around the world, visiting big cities.
     ISBN 978-1-60754-558-3 (lib.) – ISBN 978-1-60754-559-0 (pbk.)
ISBN 978-1-60754-560-6 (6-pack)
     1. Swine—Juvenile fiction 2. Travel—Juvenile fiction [1. Pigs—Fiction 2. Travel—Fiction 3. Imagination—Fiction] I. Pascoe, Pete
II. Title   III. Series
     [E]—dc22

Printed in the United States of America

For more great fiction and nonfiction, visit windmillbooks.com.

A Pig Called Pete

Written by Alan Bowater   Illustrated by Pete Pascoe

alphabet
soup™
an imprint of
WINDMILL BOOKS™
New York

Pigs are pink.

Yes?   No!

Pigs are dirty.

Yes?   No!

Pigs like mud.

Yes?   No!

Pigs can fly.

No?   Yes!

My pig Pete can fly!

Pete isn't **PINK** like ordinary, everyday pigs.

Pete is **PURPLE**

(with a **WHITE** patch around one eye).

Pete doesn't like being dirty.

He won't wallow in "icky sticky" mud ...

because it oozes between his toes and in his ears.

Pete is squeaky clean and washes
twice a day with sweet-smelling soap.

He's well groomed for a pig!

Pete's been able to fly since he was a piglet.

He flaps.

He glides.

He zooms.

He soars.

He hovers.

Every night when I go to bed

Pete flies around the world.

"Just for fun," he grunts.

Pete flies to all the big cities.

In Madrid he's a matador
and fights "El Toro," the big black bull.

In Paris he dances the cancan
at the Moulin Rouge.

In New York he bats for the Yankees
and hits a home run.

In Cairo he climbs the Great Pyramid of Giza.

In Venice he paddles a gondola
on the Grand Canal.

In London he eats cucumber sandwiches
with the Queen.

When Pete flies home he's exhausted!

I'm already awake. The morning sun streams through my bedroom window.

"Hi, Pete."

Pete just snorts!

At breakfast I tell Mom about Pete's amazing adventures.

Mom smiles and says, "but pigs can't fly!"

I tell Mom that all pigs can fly ...

...if given wings.

"Can't they, Pete?"